To my mother,
Winifred Bruce Luhrmann,
with love.

Grumpy Gloria

Grumpy Gloria

by
ANNA
DEWDNEY

SCHOLASTIC INC.
New York Toronto London Auckland
Sydney Mexico City New Delhi Hong Kong

Gloria was glum and grumpy.
Out of sorts.
Sad and lumpy.

A brand-new doll? It's time to pout!
Gloria felt so left out.

Gloria, what can we do?
Would you like a doggie chew?

Sullen, scowly, sulky, slumpy . . .
Gloria was staying grumpy.

Maybe we should brush her hair!
Little dog hairs everywhere.

Snort and snuffle, squint and scowl.
Gloria was feeling foul.

What's the matter with the dog?
Maybe she would like a jog!

Trotting,

panting,

wheezy,

dumpy . . .

Jogging made the dog **more** grumpy.

Maybe Gloria feels dirty—
get the sponge and soap and squirty!

Steamy, scrubby, slimy, soapy . . .
Gloria was mad and mopey.

Maybe she would like a toy!
Which of these would she enjoy?

Squeaky? Squawky? Jumpy? Jabby?
Gloria was feeling crabby.

Maybe she would like a game!
Dress in costume! Choose a name!

Pirate maiden, frilly-frumpy?
Gloria was **really** grumpy.

Hey, I know! She wants a ride!
Put the doggie up inside.

Weave and wobble,

scream and shout.

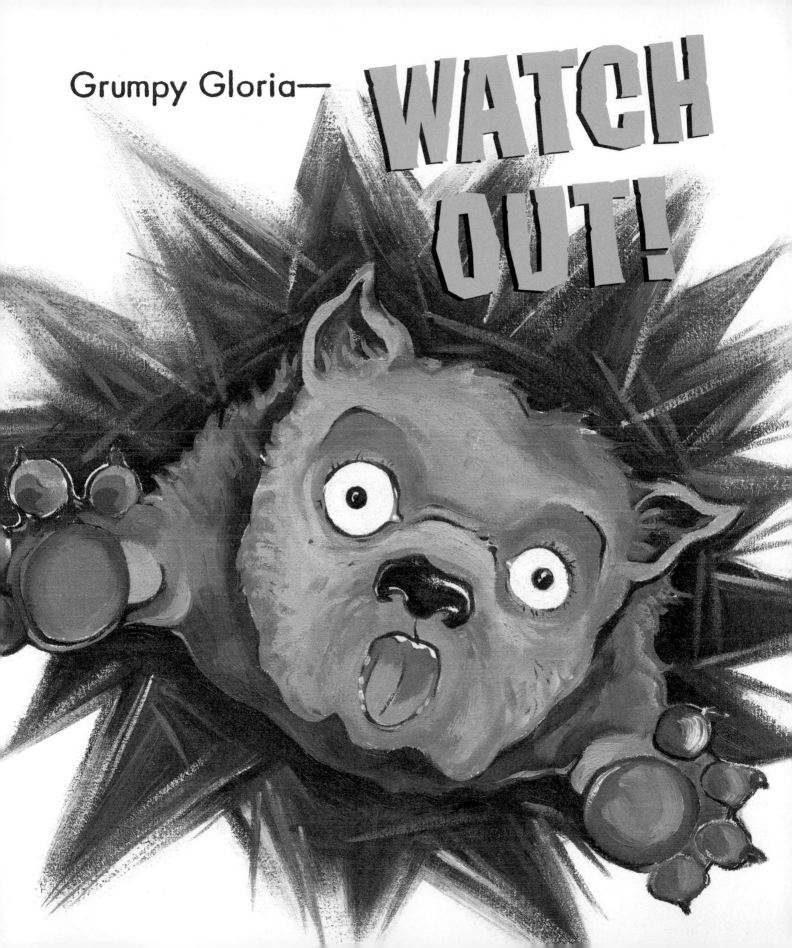

Grumpy, slumpy, gritty, grouchy.
Dirty, dusty, blinky, ouchy . . .

Wiggle-waggle.
Look! Guess who?

Gloria, there's
room for two!

Grumpy Gloria, we are done.
We're sorry you're not having fun.

But Gloria—unlike before—
wasn't grumpy . . .

. . . anymore.

ISBN 978-0-545-32860-9

12 11 10 9 8 7 6 5 4 3 2 1   11 12 13 14 15 16/0

Printed in the U.S.A.   08

First Scholastic printing, January 2011

Set in Graham
Book design by Kelley McIntyre